THE BARITONE'S PARISH

LECTOR HOUSE PUBLIC DOMAIN WORKS

This book is a result of an effort made by Lector House towards making a contribution to the preservation and repair of original classic literature. The original text is in the public domain in the United States of America, and possibly other countries depending upon their specific copyright laws.

In an attempt to preserve, improve and recreate the original content, certain conventional norms with regard to typographical mistakes, hyphenations, punctuations and/or other related subject matters, have been corrected upon our consideration. However, few such imperfections might not have been rectified as they were inherited and preserved from the original content to maintain the authenticity and construct, relevant to the work. The work might contain a few prior copyright references as well as page references which have been retained, wherever considered relevant to the part of the construct. We believe that this work holds historical, cultural and/or intellectual importance in the literary works community, therefore despite the oddities, we accounted the work for print as a part of our continuing effort towards preservation of literary work and our contribution towards the development of the society as a whole, driven by our beliefs.

We are grateful to our readers for putting their faith in us and accepting our imperfections with regard to preservation of the historical content. We shall strive hard to meet up to the expectations to improve further to provide an enriching reading experience.

Though, we conduct extensive research in ascertaining the status of copyright before redeveloping a version of the content, in rare cases, a classic work might be incorrectly marked as not-in-copyright. In such cases, if you are the copyright holder, then kindly contact us or write to us, and we shall get back to you with an immediate course of action.

HAPPY READING!

THE BARITONE'S PARISH

JAMES MEEKER LUDLOW

ISBN: 978-93-5420-305-3

Published: 1896

LECTOR HOUSE LLP
E-MAIL: lectorpublishing@gmail.com

...stood with arms interlocked and heads touching
as their voices soared in the grand finale.

THE BARITONE'S PARISH

OR
"ALL THINGS TO ALL MEN"

BY

JAMES M. LUDLOW

1896

THE BARITONE'S PARISH;
OR,
"ALL THINGS TO ALL MEN"

The pulpit and the choir gallery are closely related in our city churches. It is, however, a sad fact that the "sons of the prophets" and the "sons of Korah" usually know but little of one another; and this is to the loss of both. To the musicians the minister often seems a recluse, and the clergyman comes to look upon his choir as a band of itinerant minstrels.

It is therefore very refreshing to note that between the pastor of St. Philemon's, the Rev. Dr. Wesley Knox, and Mr. Philip Vox, there sprang up an intimacy almost from the day when the new baritone sang his first solo. It was Shelley's "Resurrection," which had been rendered as an offertory after one of the doctor's finest efforts at an Easter sermon.

Deacon Brisk, the chairman of the music committee, met the preacher at the chancel-rail within fifteen seconds after the benediction had been pronounced; before the sexton could deliver a message that a parishioner was in momentary expectation of death, and required the pastor's immediate attendance; before Lawyer Codey had adjusted his silk hat like a falcon on his wrist preparatory to his stately march down the middle aisle; and even before the soprano had adjusted her handsome face and bonnet over the front of the choir gallery to inspect the passers-out.

Deacon Brisk was like most music committee-men in that he knew little about the musical art; but he was a hustler in getting the worth of his money in whatever job he undertook. Rubbing his hands in self-congratulation upon the new baritone's engagement, he delivered himself of a panegyric which he had spent the time of the closing prayer in composing:

"I tell you, doctor, Vox was a catch. Why, he sang

> "'In slumber lay the brooding world
> Upon that glorious night,'

so sweetly that you could almost hear the stars twinkle through the music; and when he struck

> "'Let heaven's vaulted arches ring,'

it seemed as if the sky were tumbling down through the church roof. That's great singing; eh, doctor? Cost only three hundred extra; worth a thousand on the church market!"

"Yes," said the doctor, "I was pleased with the man's voice. I am impressed with the idea that there is more than larynx and training in him. There must be bigness and sweetness of soul behind those tones. Men can't sing that way to order. Come, Brisk, introduce us when those young women get through talking to him. I know I shall like him. But I didn't know that you were so well up in musical judgment."

"Why, doctor," rejoined Brisk, "it doesn't require that a man shall be an electrical engineer in order to invest successfully in a trolley."

The dominie was a bachelor. That was a pity; for a wife and family of ten could have homed themselves in his heart without detracting from the love he had for everybody else. But having no wife to console him after the efforts of a hard Sunday, he was accustomed to ask one or another of the young men to come to the study and "curry him down," as he said, after evening service.

Soon Vox came to occupy permanently this place of clerical groom. The saintly folk who thought that the light burning until Sunday midnight in the sanctum was a sign of the protracted devotions of their pastor would, on one occasion at least, have been astounded to see the reality. On the lounge was stretched the tired preacher, his feet on a pile of "skimmed" newspapers, reserved for the more thorough perusal they would never get. In his lap lay the head of a big collie, whose eyes were fixed on the handsome face of his master. Do dogs have religious instinct? If so, this was a canine hour of worship, and the dog was a genuine mystic. In some famous pictures of the adoration of the Magi less reverence and love are depicted on the faces than gleamed from beneath the shaggy eyebrows of the brute.

By the study-table sat Vox, his big bushy head and square Schiller-cut face (except for the very unpoetic mustache) bending over a chafing-dish that sent up the incense of Welsh rarebit, the ingredients of which were the offering of the landlady's piety.

"Doctor," said Vox, suddenly poising the spoon as if it were a baton, and dripping the melted cheese on to the manuscript of the night's sermon before the preacher had decided whether to put it into his "barrel" or his waste-basket—"doctor, do you know that I feel like a hypocrite, singing in a Christian church?"

"You a hypocrite, Vox? You couldn't act a false part any more than you could sing a false note without having the shivers go all through you."

"Well," replied the singer, "that is just what is the matter with me. The shivers do go through me. I am shocked at the moral discord I am making. I am striking false notes all the time. My life doesn't follow the score of my conscience. I don't mean that I have committed murder or picked pockets, but it seems to me that I am breaking the commandment by bearing false witness about myself, making people think I am a saint, or want to be one, when the fact is that I put no more heart into my singing than the organ-pipe does."

So saying Vox strode across the floor, holding a plate of rarebit as if it were a sheet of music, and jerked the toasted cheese off it as he seemed to jerk the notes off the paper when he sang.

The doctor slipped from the lounge just in time to escape a savory splash which was aiming itself straight for the space between his vest and shirt-bosom. The dog growled at the apparent attack upon his master, but was diverted from further warlike demonstrations by the bit of toast that fell under his nose.

"Your dog is as good as a special policeman for you, doctor."

"Yes, he defends me in more ways than one. Do you know why I call him Caleb? Caleb is Hebrew for 'God's dog.' One day, when he was a pup, I forgot myself and dropped into a regular pessimist over some materialistic trash I was reading. The pup seemed to notice my sour face, and put his paws upon my knees, lolled out his tongue, and searched me through and through with those bright eyes of his. It was as much as to say, 'Master, you're a fool. Look at me. Didn't it take a God to make such a marvelous creature as I am?' So I have called him Caleb ever since. He tackles many a doubt for me, as he would any other robber."

"I wish I had your faith, doctor," said Vox, putting his arm around Caleb's neck, and dropping another piece of toast into the waiting jaws.

"Faith? You have got it, Phil; only you don't know it."

"Nonsense, doctor! I suppose I believe the Creed; at least I don't disbelieve it. But I don't feel these things. That's what makes me say that I am a hypocrite to sing in a Christian church. To-night I saw a woman crying during my solo. I felt like stopping. I never feel like crying, except when the notes cry themselves; then I confess to a moistening that goes all through me. Now what right have I to make another feel what I don't feel myself? I tell you, doctor, I am nothing but a bellowing hypocrite. I'm going into opera, where it is all make-believe. You know that I've had offers that would tempt a singing devil; and I believe I would be one if it were not for you."

The doctor eyed his guest quizzically for a moment, then deliberately stretched himself again on the lounge.

"Phil, that cheese has gone to your head. I didn't think it was so strong. Yet I can understand your mistake, for I used to talk that way to myself when I was as green and unsophisticated as you are. I would scratch out the best sentences from my sermons, because I didn't feel all they meant, and would accuse myself of duplicity and cant because my experience was not up to my doctrine. But what if it wasn't? My brain isn't as big as the Bible. My conscience isn't as true and vivid as Moses' was when he wrote down the Ten Commandments. My heart isn't as tender as Christ's. If a preacher says only what he is able to feel at the moment, there will be poor fodder for the parish. So it is all through life. People talk in society on a higher level than they habitually think. They ought to. That is what society is for—to tune up to key the sagging strings of common, humdrum life. All politeness will cease when everybody acts on your theory. We must not say 'Good-morning' to a neighbor because at the moment we do not really care whether his day is going to be pleasant or not. You must not take off your hat to a lady on the street, unless at the instant you are possessed of a profound respect for the sex. Who was that composer that said that he never knew what a piece he had written until he heard Joseffy play it? They asked Parepa to sing 'Coming through the Rye.' She said, 'Pshaw! I've sung it threadbare. I grind it out now as the hand-organ does.' But she sang it, and brought down the house. Why shouldn't she? Feel! Do you suppose that old violin feels anything of the joy that thrills through its fibers? Shall I smash it for a hypocritical contrivance of wood and catgut? Did I kick Dr. Cutt out of the study the other day because he didn't realize the good he had done me in reducing the swelling of my sprained ankle? Yet you want me to let you kick yourself out of the church because you are not one of the 'angels of Jesus,' or haven't had all the joy of life crushed out of you by affliction, so that you are 'weary of earth,' as you sing!"

The doctor warmed with his theme, until, standing up, he put his big hands on Vox's shoulders, and fairly shouted at him:

"Sing, Phil! Sing the brightest, happiest things that God ever inspired men to write. But don't go croaking like an owl because you don't feel like a nightingale."

"Well," said Vox, drawing a long breath, and letting it out in a whistle, "that cheese or something else has inspired you, doctor. I never heard you so eloquent in the pulpit. Why don't you preach at us that way? Take us, as it were, one by one, and go through us, instead of preaching at humanity in the lump. I confess that you have persuaded me about my Sunday work. I am not going to leave it off. But now for the other six days in the week. I can convince you that they are full of husks that do nobody any good. Here's my diary. Isn't it contemptible for a man with even a singer's conscience? Monday, sung at Checkley's musicale for fifty dollars and a score of feminine compliments; Tuesday, in oratorio for one hundred dollars and some newspaper puffs, which were all wrong from a critical stand-point; Wednesday, moped all day because I couldn't sing—raw throat; Thursday, made believe teach a lot of tone-deaf fellows who can never sing any more than crows, and took their money for the imposition; Friday, ditto; Saturday, rehearsal. Now who am I helping by peddling my chin-wares?"

Vox stopped for lack of breath, as well as from the fact that his week had run out.

"Go on," said the doctor, nonchalantly. "You can certainly slander yourself worse than that. What! no more? Why, Vox, I know there are worse things about you than what you have told me."

Vox colored.

"You needn't blush so over it, Phil," and the doctor burst out laughing at him. "I am not going to twit you on any disagreeable facts. I didn't say I knew what those worse things were; but I do know that you are not such a sweet saint as to have only the faults mentioned. If they were all, I would have a glass case made for you at once, put your bones up in leather, and place a basin of holy water at your door for passers-by to dip their fingers in. But soberly, Phil, I think I can size you up, or down."

"All right; try it. You may find me so big a fool that it will take some time to get my full measurement."

With that he stretched himself to his full height, and posed with his fingers in his vest-holes. The attitude interested Caleb, who stretched himself out to almost corresponding dimensions horizontally along the floor, recovering his legs slowly to the accompaniment of a long and dismal whine.

"He does that," said the doctor, "only when there is going to be a death in the neighborhood, or when I begin to read my sermons aloud in the study. He knows I am going to lecture you. Charge, Caleb!

"Dearly beloved Vox! you have two first-class deficiencies. First, a purposeless life. You happen to be doing good with that wonderful voice of yours; but that is nothing to your credit. You can't help cheering people when you wag your jaws any more than Caleb can help being a comfort to me when he wags his tail. You didn't study music for the sake of helping anybody, but only because music gave you a pleasurable means of getting a livelihood. So you have no soul-satisfaction in your profession, for all you are succeeding so grandly in it. You are like that piece of music which you said was a failure, because, though there were some fine harmonies in it, it had no theme, no prevailing idea, no musical purpose."

"That's me," said Vox, *sotto voce*, holding his head in his hands. "I know that I am a mere medley, part sacred, part profane, and both parts played by the devil! Go on."

"Stop your pessimism," rejoined the doctor. "That poetic head of yours reminds me that Schiller in the 'Bell' gives utterance to the same idea I am trying to beat into you."

"The Bell? That's me, too; all brass and clapper!" grumbled Vox, twisting Caleb's ears until the brute whined.

The doctor, not heeding either the singer's soliloquy or the brute's, quoted in oratorical style:

> "'So let us duly ponder all
> The works our feeble strength achieves;
> For mean, in truth, the man we call
> Who ne'er what he completes conceives.
>
> And well it stamps our human race,
> And hence the gift to understand,
> That man within the heart should trace
> Whate'er he fashions with the hand.'"

Vox groaned. "That's rather heavy poetry for creatures of our caliber, isn't it, Caleb? But I guess that I catch on.—It means the same as the line of the hymn you gave out to-night, doctor;" and Vox sang:

> "'Take my voice, and let me sing
> Always, only, for my King.'

"That is, if I'm a bell, I should be one on purpose, whether a church-bell, or a door-bell, or only 'God's dog,' to growl"—patting Caleb. "But what is that second thing I lack? Since you've taken the contract to make me over, I want you to be thorough with the job."

"The second thing you need," said the doctor, "is in some way to be made to see that you are doing good. From your perch in the gallery you don't get a glimpse into the people's hearts. I couldn't preach if I didn't go among the people during the week, and get the encouragement of knowing that I had helped somebody."

"Yes," said Vox, "I've heard Joe Jefferson say that he couldn't act worth a cent if the people didn't applaud. I beg your pardon, doctor, for comparing the pulpit with the stage. But go on with your lecture."

"Oh, you've knocked the lecture out of my head with your nonsense, Phil."

"But you knocked it pretty well into mine. I'd like to see somebody I've helped. Show him up."

"Humph!" grunted the doctor, and, after a moment's silence, said abruptly, "Phil, will you go with me to-morrow night?"

"Where?"

"Leave that to me."

"That's a blind sort of an invitation, doctor. But, of course, I will go anywhere you want me to. But what is it? Some holy Sorosis? That reformed theater you talk about? Any charge for admittance, or collection? Of course, going with a distinguished clergyman I shall have to appear in swallow-tails and arctic shirt-front."

"Not a bit of it, Phil; your oldest clothes, so that you will look just as mean as you say you feel; then, for once, you can't accuse yourself of being a hypocrite."

There was a motley crowd in the front room of a Bowery twenty-cent lodging-house. The room was the parlor, but the occupants called it the "deck," in distinction from the rest of the house, which was filled with bunks. There were hard old soakers in a periodical state of repentance; or, to speak more scientifically, in that state of gland-moistening that comes after a certain amount of poor beer has permeated the system. There were young prodigals, in there for the night because they had no money for a night's carousal elsewhere. There was a sprinkling of honest men, thankful for even this refuge from the sleety streets. There were some two hundred pieces of the great human wreck made by the hard times, which were beached in Brady's Harbor, as the place was called.

The usual hubbub had calmed while a story-teller, who sat on the edge of a table, and whose slouch-hat and high ulster collar did not altogether conceal the genial face of Dr. Knox, entertained the crowd with old army yarns, which, as usual with such literature, were taken largely from the apocryphal portion of our national annals.

"Bully for you! Give us another!" was the encore, emphasized with the rattle of backgammon-boards and boot-heels.

"Haven't any more; but I have a friend here who will bring up the reserves in the way of a song."

"Song, song! Rosin your larynx, old boy!" greeted the suggestion, while the crowd gathered closer about Vox, and several who had "turned in" for the night turned out of their bunks again, minus coats and boots. A friendly slap on the back by something less than a ten-pound hand helped the singer to clear his throat.

Vox gave them "O'Grady's Goat" and one or two other classics of the Tenderloin district, with the rapt appreciation of his audience. Tom Moore's "Minstrel Boy," to the genuine old Irish melody, struck the heroic chord in the breasts of men most of whom were deserters from the real battle-fields of life. Then Vox dropped into a lullaby. The tender mother words given in his masculine tones seemed a burlesque as he began; but the deep bass took on the softness and sweetness of a contralto, and made one think, if not of a mother cooing to her baby, at least of some rough, great-hearted man who had found a lost child and was rocking it to sleep in his strong arms. More than one greasy sleeve got into its owner's eyes before Vox ended.

"An' 'aven't ye a Scotch sang, me laddie?" asked an old fellow, knocking the ashes from his pipe against the window-sill.

"My Ain Countrie" followed. As the music floated, the thick smoke of the room seemed to drift away. The land of birds and beauty lay before eyes that for months and years had looked only upon the crowded misery of slumdom. When the voice ceased the illusion continued for a while in spite of the picking sleet at the window-panes.

At length the silence was broken by a voice that came from a distant corner of the room. It repeated the last verse in tones as pure as those of Vox himself, though a high tenor in quality. Some of the notes were broken by hiccups.

Vox looked in amazement at the singer — a half-drunken youngish man curled nearly double in a chair which was tipped back against the wall. His battered derby and unscraped chin did not effectually disguise the handsome fellow beneath them. He was like the Apollo Belvedere when first exhumed from the mud of Antium.

"Who are you, my friend?" asked Vox, in as kindly a tone as his surprise allowed.

"Friend? (hic) haven't got any friend," replied the man; and he struck up the verse that had just been rendered. His voice was husky at first, but after a few notes it clarified itself, as brooks do in running. His tones became marvelously sweet, touching the highest note without the slightest suggestion of falsetto. It was a transcendent voice, one that might have once belonged to some spirit, and gone astray among men. The singer went through the verse this time without hiccup or slur; but the instant he stopped the drunk resumed its sway. Down came the chair with a bump on to its front legs, which sent the man headlong into the arms of Vox, with whom he wanted to fight.

"I won't fight you," said Vox, helping him back to his seat; "but I'll dare you to sing with me."

"Sin' wi' you! 'Cept your challenge. I can whip you with my—my tongue (hic) as bad as my wife she (hic) whipped me with her (hic) tongue."

"What shall we sing, old boy?" inquired Vox, with that easy familiarity which showed that he had seen such customers before.

> "Sin' a song o' sispence,
> Pocket full o' rye,"

sang the man. "Say, what's the use o' havin' your pocket full o' rye (hic)? 'D rather have a belly full o' rye; wouldn't you (hic)?"

"You've enough rye in you for to-night," said Vox. "Come, pull the cork out of your throat, and let's have a song."

Vox got a chair, and tipped it back by the side of the maudlin fellow, then struck up Mazzini's two-part song, "The Muleteers." The stranger joined in. Such singing was never heard before nor since in Brady's Harbor, nor, for that matter, in Carnegie Hall. After a bar or two the men rose to their feet and stood with arms interlocked and heads touching as their voices soared in the grand finale.

The noise brought in Brady, who said it was "galoreous," but for all that they'd have to "bolt up their chins," as it was past twelve o'clock, and the "perlice wasn't so easy on lodgin'-houses as they was on the swill-shops."

"See here, Vox," said the doctor, "I am going home alone to-night. Find out your pal. Chum him a bit. A man with that voice has had culture. Scrape the rust off him, and you will find something polished beneath, or I am no judge of human nature. Take him for your parish, Phil."

"A heathenish sort of a mission that," replied Vox, looking at the fellow, who was trying, as he said, to find his night-key to get his boots off with. After a moment's hesitation, Vox added: "All right, doctor; you've had as hard a field with me, if it wasn't so dirty a one. I'll take him for a sobering walk in the drizzle, and then get him into better quarters than he has here."

Vox had his hands full with his job, and at times his arms full too. His companion insisted that the Bowery sidewalk, covered with sleet, was a toboggan-slide, and that he was tumbling off the sled. What could Vox do with his protégé? He couldn't walk him or slide him all night. A policeman proposed to relieve him of his anxiety by taking them both to the station-house, but was persuaded not to perform this heroic exploit by the man's assurance that his pal's legs hadn't any snakes in them, and by Vox's demonstration that he could stand alone. Then Vox thought of the story of the good Samaritan, with rising respect for the priest that passed by on the other side. Next, having got into the charity business, he envied the Samaritan at least his ass, "instead," as Vox soliloquized, "of making an ass of myself." He thought of taking the fellow to some hotel, paying for his lodging, and hiring the clerk to see that he was properly sobered off in the morning; but concluded that, whatever might have been the case on the road to Jericho, there was no innkeeper on the Bowery whom he could trust with such a commission, or who would trust him to call in the morning and pay the bill. He could take him back to Brady's Harbor, he thought; but when they turned about the man declared that he wouldn't walk up a toboggan-slide, and sat down on the sidewalk for another ride.

The flash of a passing cab let a little light in upon his problem. Hailing the driver, with whose help he got his load into the vehicle, he told him to drive to No. — Madison Avenue, where he had his own day quarters—elegant rooms, fitted up for his instruction of the fashionable "daughters of music" at six dollars an hour. Sweezy, the janitor, was roused up, and with his assistance Vox was able to congratulate himself that he had gone "one better" on the good Samaritan, in that he had lodged his man in finer chambers. He could not help laughing at the incongruousness of the snoring mass and the elegant divan on which it lay. He thought of Bottom the weaver, with the ass's head, in the lap of Titania, and, as he piled the cushions so that the fellow would not tumble off, addressed him in the words of the fairy:

> "Come, sit thee down upon this flowery bed,
> While I thy amiable cheeks do coy,
> And stick musk roses in thy sleek smooth head,
> And kiss thy fair large ears, my gentle joy."

But tears are near to laughter, and as Vox contemplated his completed work he had to sit down a moment and cry.

"It's a hard sight, sir," said Sweezy, "but bless you, Mr. Vox, the best of us has just sich among our closest friends. I wish, sir, as how it was my own boy, Tommy, you had found the night." And Sweezy cried too.

Sweezy promised to take an early look at the man in the morning when he turned on the steam heat. Vox went away to his boarding-house around the corner, vexed at the doctor for getting him into such a scrape, yet feeling down in the depths of his heart a satisfaction that more than half compensated him for his rough experience. He fell asleep thinking of the good Samaritan, Bottom with the ass's head, Salvation Army lasses, and the Prohibition party; and, in the midst of a horrid dream, woke up imagining himself drunk and about to fall off a precipice.

Before breakfast next morning he went around to the rooms to look after his charge. The fellow had vamosed. Sweezy was taking account of the furniture, and, though nothing was missing, and only a lamp-shade broken, declared that Vox had been victimized by a sharper:

"A regular sharper, sir. I thought so when you brought him in. You ought to have knowed, sir, at a glance of him, what he was. You've nussed, sir, a wiper in your bosom, and it's a mercy, sir, a mercy if he hasn't stung you no worse. Is your pocket-book with you? You ought at least to have took off his boots. That spot on the cover will never come out without piecing."

Vox contemplated the scene of his first charity exploit much as Bonaparte did the battle-field of Waterloo. He had but one remark to make, which was:

"Sweezy, don't you open your head about this business."

Vox was not in an amiable mood when he met the doctor the next Sunday night. He debated with him the inadvisability of decent people attempting to do slumming in the name of either religion or charity. He took the ground that the men who had themselves been rescued from the dens of the city were the only ones to do this work, as they train chetahs to hunt their own kind, and reformed thieves to become detectives.

The doctor was half inclined to agree with him, not so much from conviction as from seeing the disgust the business had wrought in the mind of his friend. Yet he excused himself for having led Vox into this experience on the ground that it is Christian duty to try to rescue the fallen, even though one does not accomplish anything.

"I don't believe in your theory," said Vox, warmly. "Let buzzards clean up the offal, but decent birds had better follow their sweeter instincts and keep away. One thing is certain: I am not going to light on such moral carrion again."

It was more than a month later when a respectable-looking stranger called upon Vox at his rooms. The singer was engaged at the time arranging with a lady of the Four Hundred for the vocal culture of her daughters. The visitor quietly awaited his leisure. He was very genteel in appearance. If one had been critical he might have thought that for such a stinging cold day an ulster would have been more suitable than the light fall overcoat he wore; and some might have observed that it was not the fashion that season to wear one's outer garment so short that the tails of the under-coat protruded. But Vox was occupied with the stranger's face, which was exceedingly prepossessing.

"Mr. Vox, I believe?"

"My name, sir. What can we do for each other?"

"If I am not mistaken in the person, you once did me a great service."

"You must be mistaken in the person," said Vox, "or else I have done it unconsciously, for I have no recollection of our having met."

The man seemed puzzled. "Possibly!" he said, slowly, as he scanned the singer's features.

"Undoubtedly it is so," said Vox, and, seeing the man's perplexity, quickly added, in the most genial manner, "I am sorry it is so, for I should be glad to remember that I had served you. Possibly I may do so in the future."

The man hesitatingly began to withdraw. Near the door he stopped, and, glancing about the room, half to himself and half as an apology to Vox, said, "Perhaps I have dreamed it. But will you allow me to ask you a question? Do you ever sing Mazzini's 'Muleteers'?"

"Often," replied Vox. "This, you mean," and he struck up the first line. His visitor instantly joined him. Vox stopped as quickly.

"Good heavens!" he exclaimed. "There are not two voices in the world like that." Putting his hand on the man's shoulder, he peered into his face. He could not recall the features, for the dim light in Brady's Harbor and the general slouch of the fellow that night had not really allowed him to see his face fully. He imagined how this man might look with a week's beard on his chin, an untrimmed mustache covering his fine lips, and a dirty derby concealing his forehead.

"Are you that man?"

"I am; or, rather, I was that man. But I hope—thanks to God and you—I am a very different man to-day. I came to tell you my gratitude for a kindness which I had come to doubt one man ever rendered to another, and to apologize for my bestial treatment of you. I was not a man then, Mr. Vox, only a beast; and, if you will believe me, I was not accountable, for I knew no better. I have the vaguest remembrance of that night, as of many another night. When I awoke at daylight in these rooms I had just sense enough to know that somebody had befriended me or played a trick on me, and to be ashamed to meet him, whoever he was. So I sneaked away. When I was sobered I couldn't recall the place. But the 'Muleteers' rang in my ears, and your voice, every note, the tone and quality. I had heard you sing elsewhere, and knew that but one voice, that of Vox, could have sung in that way. And now it has taken a month for me to get up manliness enough to come and do the decent thing."

"Don't talk in that way," said Vox, coloring as if he were receiving abuse instead of praise. "I did nothing that any man would not do for another. A man would be inhuman, a mere brute, not to—"

Then he thought of what he had lately said to the doctor about buzzards and benevolent slummers, and he felt like a hypocrite again.

"But don't talk about the past. Let it go. Isn't there something I can do for you now?" glancing at the man's threadbare coat.

"Yes, there is one favor I would like very much to have you do me. I have had a hard struggle with myself these few weeks. I resolved that I would not drink again. I have kept my purpose, but it has been like being tied to a wild beast in a cage. More than once I have started out for a drink, but have come back without it. It is hard to feel that you are all alone in the fight, that nobody knows of it. It's like making that cane stand by itself."

"But you have friends," said Vox, kindly.

"Friends that have ceased to be friends are worse than strangers," replied the man, in an abstracted sort of way. "My friends don't believe in me; I've got to make new friends, who don't know how weak I am. Perhaps they will believe in me for a while at least, and that will give a man some strength. But to be all alone in a fearful struggle! Oh, it's the loneliness that takes all the heart out of one. You know how one voice steadies another in singing. Drunk as I was when I sang with you, I believe I sang every note correctly; but alone I couldn't have rendered three notes true. I want you to let me rest for a while on your confidence, your good wishes, Mr. Vox; and to let me drop in once in a while, just to tell you that I am all right yet."

"My good fellow, you can come, and you can stay with me just as much as you want to," said Vox; and for all that he knew that this was a very rash thing to say to a stranger, he would have resented any one's telling him so.

"No," replied the man, "I shall not intrude upon you; but may I ask you to keep this pledge I have written? The paper is crumpled; that's because I have taken it out so often when the temptation was pretty strong. It was something like a friend; and I could say to it, 'You see I have kept faith with you, bit of paper, and I will.' So I would start out on another campaign. But if you will keep it for me I will feel better. I can think then that somebody knows what I am doing."

Vox took the paper. It was written in fine penmanship, and signed "Charles Downs."

"Downs? Charles Downs? Not Downs who used to be in the Mendelssohn? The tenor at St. Martha's? And you are speaking of being grateful to me for a common act of humanity! Why, man, I owe more to you than I can ever repay. It was hearing you sing once that gave me my first ambition to be a singer. I began to save my money that night that I might take lessons. I even tried to find you; but you had gone, nobody knew where."

"I was on the road to hell then," said Downs. "Thank Heaven you didn't find me; I might have injured you by my example. But no, I think not. You were not inclined my way."

The two men sat in silence for a few moments. Thought was becoming oppressive. Vox was of that mercurial disposition that cannot keep solemn long at a time. His vent-valves worked easily.

"Come," said he, "let's try the old song."

If he had deliberated he would not have chosen a reminder of the past. But there was something irresistible about Vox, and Downs joined with him as they rollicked through the "Muleteers."

Sweezy stood in the doorway listening.

"That," said Vox, "is the greatest compliment a man can have. Sweezy there has no more music in him than a horse; but see! we have woven the spell about him. I believe we do sing well together. What couldn't we do if we would practise together? Now I will keep this pledge for you, Downs, if you will promise to come every day at twelve and sing with me. We will lunch together, and I will see that you don't get a drop to drink."

"I can't."

"Why not?"

"I have engaged to go to work."

"Where?"

"Enlisted."

"What! Enlisted? To throw yourself away again?" Vox gripped the arms of Downs as if he were a prisoner. "Where have you enlisted?"

"In the street-sweeping brigade."

"Great guns!" said Vox.

"No, great brooms!" replied his friend. "I need outdoor work; there I will get it. I need to keep away from other men; and on the street I will be left to my own company as nicely as if I were a hermit. Besides, there will be a poetic fitness in one who has lived so dirty a life as I have giving himself up to the work of cleaning things. Then, too, I can see life; and that will be interesting. Nothing is so fascinating to one who has had my experience as the sight of a crowd, if only one can himself keep out of it." With that Downs sang:

> "'Hurry along, sorrow and song;
> All is vanity under the sun.
> Velvet and rags: so the world wags,
> Until the river no more shall run.'"

Vox readily upset the street-sweeping project by showing Downs how he could be helpful to him in certain musical matters he had on foot, and even guaranteed to turn over to him several of his pupils who were trying to develop tenor voices.

The next Sunday night after service the doctor took the singer's arm at the church door with his usual chirpy invitation, "Come, Phil, don't let Mrs. Cupp's pepper and mustard get cold, or the cheese get away from us."

"Walk around the block with me first, doctor; I've got something to tell you which I'd rather you would hear when you can't see my face."

"Why, what have you been doing now that you are ashamed of, Phil? Oh, I know. You have proposed to the soprano, or been perpetrating some other trick on your bachelor friends. I'll forgive you at the start, however, because"—lowering his voice until there was a frog in it—"because I know something about—but it's none of your business, Phil, so I won't tell you anything about it. No disappointment, my boy?"

"No."

"Then count on me to marry you for nothing, and throw in the benediction besides."

"It's no love-affair," said Vox. "Cupid might as well break his arrows on a rhinoceros as shoot at me. It's that drunken fellow. I've been awfully taken in."

"What! has he turned up? Fleeced you again?"

"Well, not exactly fleeced me, but scorched me; he has heaped coals of fire on my head. I want to take back all I have said against him, and everything I said against slumming."

He then related what the reader knows. Having worked off the steam of his extra emotion, he accompanied the doctor to the study. Here Vox gave a description of his new friend: "a well-educated man, a splendid all-round musician, a fine business man; has a wife who won't live with him, nor even let him see her—he has treated her so outrageously; but he loves her tenderly. He was once employed by Silver & Co., who thought so much of him that they were making proposals for his entering the firm when they began to suspect his rum habit. His name is

Downs."

"Downs? With Silver & Co.?" The names set the doctor thinking. At length, coming out of his reverie, he picked up from the study-table a piece of marble, a bit of a fluted column he had found amid the ruins of the Temple of Diana at Ephesus. He traced on it with the pen the word D-o-w-n-s. Then he rubbed the word out with his finger; but a black spot was left that he could not get off the marble.

"There! that's the way I would spoil the job if I should try to restore the ruins of Downs. Phil, stick to that man. I'll leave him to you. He's your parish. With your voice and his love of music, you ought to make him follow you as the rocks followed Orpheus. That's the meaning of the old legend—you can sing the hardest wretch into heaven. Try it, Phil."

The doctor spent a half-hour next day in Silver & Co.'s office. Just what he and Silver talked about we cannot say; but Silver was overheard to remark, as the doctor was leaving, "My wife thinks the world of the little woman, and when those two women are satisfied with his reformation, all right."

There never was a finer program for a musicale than that which, some six months later, packed the upper Carnegie Hall with the elite of the music-lovers of New York. Vox was the drawing card, for he had become, if not the celebrity, at least the fad, of the season. "Oh, Vox! he's just splendid!" was as familiarly heard as the clicking of afternoon tea-cups everywhere between Flushing and Orange Mountain. On the occasion referred to he had achieved a sevenfold encore for one performance. To the surprise of everybody, however, when he appeared to acknowledge the ovation, he led another man with him to the footlights; one who might have been his twin brother, for there was just that sort of difference between them that ought to exist between a tenor and a baritone—the former a little slighter in form and features. Curiosity was not allowed to get to the whispering-point when they rendered the Graben-Hoffman duet, "I feel thy angel spirit."

The applause was furious. Nothing like it had been heard for six months outside of Brady's Harbor. Vox gracefully stepped a little to the rear. The audience caught his meaning, and the room rang with the cry of "Tenor! tenor!"

Vox slipped to the piano, and played the chords of "Salva di Mora" from Gounod's "Faust." And how grandly Downs sang it! If Deacon Brisk had been there, even he, with his "star-twinkling" and "roof-splitting" metaphors, could not have described it.

"If Faust sang like that," said an elderly gentleman in the audience to his wife, "no wonder he won the heart of Marguerite." And he pressed his wife's hand, which somehow had got into his.

"Hush, John," replied the woman. Then she put a handkerchief to her eyes instead of her lorgnette.

"He's all right again," said the man, and he squeezed his wife's arm, and nudged her nervously.

"John, don't!" And the woman glanced at the woman next to her, as if that individual might care what cooing these old doves indulged in.

This other woman wore a half-veil, one of those vizors with which women hide their beauty or their freckles from the gaze of the curious. Not seeing her face, one cannot say what was transpiring behind the veil; but the veil shook as if some convulsive emotion might be working itself out, or struggling to keep itself in.

When Downs left the stage Vox hugged him as a bear would her cub. "Come," said he, "let's go out in the room and talk to the Silvers."

"The Silvers here!" exclaimed Downs, in consternation.

"They were here, but I believe they have left. Yes, their seats are empty. Now that's too bad."

"No wonder they left when they saw me on the stage. Vox, you know that they know all about me. They would kick me off their doorstep if I were a beggar. You've disgraced yourself by bringing me here, as I told you you would. The Silvers, of all the people in the world! I wouldn't have sung if I had suspected their being here."

"Well, you did sing. Thank God for it, too," replied his friend.

The next Sunday night at the hobnob Vox tried to make a report to the doctor of the progress of his protégé.

"Oh, he sang magnificently! I tell you, that man is reinstated in this community. Do you know, doctor, the Silvers were both there?"

"Indeed!" ejaculated his friend, pulling Caleb's tail, and laughing at the dog's surprise. Then he pulled it again, and laughed at the dog's jump as if he had never seen such antics before.

"See here, doctor, you don't seem to care about Downs. That dog is more to you than a human being. But you've got to listen to me."

Vox got rapturous in his account of Downs's success, and ended with, "I couldn't help wishing that his wife had been there to see him—handsome, healthy, true man in every feature and tone of voice. She would have had to fall in love again, or I'll forswear all faith in the sex."

The doctor rolled himself on the sofa in such glee that the dog accepted his master's antics as a challenge to more of his own, and pounced upon him.

"What's the matter with you now?" asked the singer, in amazement.

"Why, his wife was there," roared the doctor.

"The thunder she was!" Vox jumped up as if he had been sitting in an electric chair.

Caleb growled to hear such language in the presence of his patron saint.

"I beg your pardon, doctor, but how do you know she was there?"

"Why, I suppose she was, because Mrs. Silver promised to go and take her to hear *you* sing." And the doctor laughed so loud and hilariously that the collie crept under the lounge, as if in fear of some more serious explosion.

"And you have been playing the hypocrite with me all the time?" Vox was nettled. "If I had known that I wouldn't have sung a note, nor would I have let Downs do it, either."

"Yet you just said you wish she had been there. Don't you see that had you known you would have spoiled your own job?" said the doctor, working out of his hysteria. "But, Phil, I'm hungry with preaching and laughing at you. Light up the chafing-dish, put in plenty of red pepper, and when your cockles are warmed you may read this," tossing him a note.

Vox read:

> "DEAR DOCTOR: When I heard Downs sing the other night, I felt sure that your judgment of him was correct, and that he is a new man. Mrs. Downs has been with him for several days. God bless that little woman! She has borne up bravely during her trial; never lost heart; and now she has her reward. Of course Downs has his old place with us. I want to know that Mr. Vox. Bring him around to dine with us Wednesday night. If my wife can persuade them, we will have Mr. and Mrs. Downs too.
>
> "Yours faithfully,
> "JOHN SILVER."

While Vox was reading the note Caleb came out from under the lounge, and putting his head in the singer's lap, gazed as worshipfully into his face as he had ever gazed into that of his master.

Lector House believes that a society develops through a two-fold approach of continuous learning and adaptation, which is derived from the study of classic literary works spread across the historic timeline of literature records. Therefore, we aim at reviving, repairing and redeveloping all those inaccessible or damaged but historically as well as culturally important literature across subjects so that the future generations may have an opportunity to study and learn from past works to embark upon a journey of creating a better future.

This book is a result of an effort made by Lector House towards making a contribution to the preservation and repair of original ancient works which might hold historical significance to the approach of continuous learning across subjects.

HAPPY READING & LEARNING!

LECTOR HOUSE LLP
E-MAIL: lectorpublishing@gmail.com